# STAYING NINE

*Pam Conrad*

# STAYING NINE

*Illustrated By*
*Mike Wimmer*

————HARPER & ROW, PUBLISHERS————
*Cambridge, Philadelphia,*
*San Francisco, St. Louis,*
*London, Singapore, Sydney*
*New York*

Staying Nine
Text copyright © 1988 by Pam Conrad
Illustrations copyright © 1988 by Mike Wimmer
Printed in the U.S.A. All rights reserved.
Typography by Andrew Rhodes
1  2  3  4  5  6  7  8  9  10
First Edition

Library of Congress Cataloging-in-Publication Data
Conrad, Pam.
    Staying nine.

    Summary: Nine-year-old Heather doesn't want to
turn ten until wacky Rosa Rita shows her that growing
up isn't so bad.
    [1. Growth—Fiction.  2. Birthdays—Fiction]
I. Title.  II. Title: Staying 9.
PZ7.C76476St  1988        [Fic]        87-45862
ISBN 0-06-021319-1
ISBN 0-06-021320-5 (lib. bdg.)

*for Sarah*

*I Don't Live Here!*
*Prairie Songs*
*Holding Me Here*
*What I Did for Roman*
*Seven Silly Circles*
*Taking the Ferry Home*

# 1
# Being Nine
# Forever and Ever

It was a cold November day, a week before Heather's birthday, and the house was warm with cooking and good smells. Heather was in the kitchen alone, putting away the last of her homework and feeling a little restless, when the old urge came over her. She stopped what she was doing and stood in the doorway to the dining room.

Heather pressed her hands against the moldings, hands dry and fingers down. She gave herself a little lift, and then pressed the bottoms of her sneakers against the inside of the doorway as well. Bit by bit, hands, feet, hands, feet, Heather inched her way up the wall until her shoulders were touching the very top of the doorway and her head was resting back on the molding.

"Heather, isn't it your day to set the table?" her mother asked, passing underneath Heather and between her sneakers like a ship passing beneath a bridge.

"Nope," Heather answered. "It's Sam's turn today." Sam was her older sister.

"Well, Samantha won't be here tonight. She's having dinner at Amy's, so why don't you do it now, and she'll take your turn tomorrow?"

"But I did it yesterday! That's two days in a row!"

Mrs. Fitz stopped short and looked up at her. "You know, you're right! That's unfair. Why, I cooked dinner yesterday, and here I am doing it again." Mrs. Fitz slipped the apron from around her waist and tossed it over the back of the chair. "Forget this nonsense. I'm going dancing."

Heather watched in amazement from her high perch as her mother reached for her coat on the hook, slipped into it, and disappeared out the back door. "Ma!" But she was gone. Heather eased her pressure on the wall and slid slowly down the moldings until her feet were on the floor. She threw on her coat, not even bothering to zip it up, and ran out the back door. "Ma!"

Her mother was walking up the gravel driveway, lugging the big green garbage can. Heather caught up to her and took one of the handles. "Where are you going?"

"To the curb," her mother answered.

"I thought you said you were going dancing."

Her mother smiled at her and shrugged. "Changed my mind."

Heather smiled back. "You're going to cook dinner, right?"

They set the can down at the curb. "Are you going to set the table?" her mother asked.

Heather nodded.

"Well, I guess I'll cook then and keep you company."

The sky was pink across the street, and Heather and her mother both looked up at it. Heather slipped her hand into her mother's. "It's the same sunset every night, isn't it?" asked Heather.

"What do you mean?"

"I mean it always goes down over the Boggses' house, and it always makes the sky all different colors. How come it never goes down over the Palmers' house, or down in our backyard?"

"It's the rotation of the earth, *you* know that. Up in the east, down in the west. That's just the way it is, for millions of years. It's always the same."

"I wish I could stay just the same for millions of years," Heather said. "Don't you wish you could just stand here like this, and never change?"

Her mother looked at her. "What made you think that, Heather?"

She shrugged. "I don't know. I'm just feeling glad to be nine. I think I want to stay like this. Exactly as I am today."

" 'As clever as clever'?"

Heather laughed. She remembered the old Winnie-the-Pooh poem. "That's right, but I think I'll be *nine* now forever and ever."

They walked back to the house up the long driveway. Her mother slipped her arm around Heather, and Heather noticed she came to her mother's shoulder already. She was growing. There was nothing she could do about it, and she suddenly felt a sinking feeling inside. She turned to look back at the sky over the Boggses' house. It had changed, too, and now there were streaks of gold clouds in the trees.

The house was warm to return to, and smelled wonderful to Heather. She set the table for her mother and herself, being careful to turn the dishes so the design of the Chinese house and the birds was right side up.

"We should plan your birthday party tonight, Heather," her mother said, pulling the pan of chicken out of the oven and setting it on the stove. "It's only seven days away."

Heather stood very still, a thought coming to her. "I don't want a birthday this year," she said quietly.

Her mother went on as if Heather hadn't said that. "We'll have Grandma and Grandpa, and Uncle Lou and his girlfriend, and you can invite a few of your friends from school, and—"

"I don't want a party this year. I'm going to skip it."

"But why?" Mrs. Fitz poured the pot of boiling noodles into a colander in the sink, and steam enveloped her and clouded up the windows.

"I'm going to stay nine awhile longer. I'm not ready for ten."

Mrs. Fitz laughed. "It doesn't work that way, toots. Believe me, if it did, I would have stopped myself around twenty-four." She shook the colander over the sink. "Ah, to have the energy I had then! And the hips!"

Heather felt the urge again and backed up to the doorway, where she braced her arms against the molding and scooted back up to her perch near the ceiling. "I'm not ready," she said. "That's all. No party."

"What will we tell everybody?" her mother asked, peering up at her. "You know Grandpa always gives you a dollar for each year you are, and I always make that pink lemonade cake and the moon cookies."

"Just tell them we're skipping it this year." Heather's eyes began to fill with tears.

Her mother looked up at her thoughtfully. "You're serious, aren't you?"

She nodded.

"But I love your birthday," Mrs. Fitz said.

"No you don't. You always cry at seven forty-five."

Her mother smiled. "It's because I'm so happy, that's all. I like to remember the very moment you were born. It makes me so happy, I cry. I can't help it."

"Tell me about when I was a baby," Heather said, beginning to feel hungry as the chicken and the steaming buttered noodles were laid out on the table. She slowly slid back down to the floor and took her seat.

"You were delicious," her mother said. "And fat!"

"How fat?" She knew the answer before her mother even said it.

"A moon."

She was so fat, her mother called her *Moon*, and that was why she baked those moon cookies every year on her birthday.

"You can bake moon cookies next week," Heather said, "but no birthday party. I mean it."

"You really *do* mean it, don't you?"

"Yes." Heather concentrated on cutting her crunchy chicken. "No party. No candles. No presents. No singing. No ten years old. I'm staying nine."

"But Heather—"

Heather put her hands over her ears and started to hum. She watched her mother, and when her mother stopped talking and started to cut her own chicken, Heather took her hands down and went back to eating. And that, thought Heather, was the end of that.

# 2
# Exactly the Same
# as Last Year

The next night Heather was sitting in her closet with her flashlight, reading a ghost story. She had made a soft nest for herself out of quilts and pillows, and it was very quiet—dark and private.

"Heather?"

She heard her mother knocking on the door to her room. Then the door squeaked open and her mother called again. "Heather?"

"I'm in my office," Heather answered, frowning now that she was discovered and interrupted.

The door opened wide, and Heather shone the flashlight on her mother's face. "What are you doing?" her mother asked, shielding her eyes with some clean shirts and sweaters she was holding by their hangers.

"I'm reading," Heather answered, turning the light back on her book and trying to find her place.

"Isn't it stuffy in here?" Her mother hung Heather's clothes above her on the rod.

"I like it," Heather said simply, snuggling down even deeper into her nest.

Mrs. Fitz smiled. "You always did," she said softly. "I remember when you were real little, you'd climb into any box and go to sleep. For a while there, that was the *only* way you'd go to sleep. Even when you were new-born, you'd fuss and move until your blanket would cover your face, and then you'd quiet down. What a funny kid you were."

"Did you wash my pink shirt?" Heather asked, suddenly feeling a little uncomfortable. "Tomorrow's picture day, and Dorelle and I promised to wear the same shirt, so we can be like twins."

Mrs. Fitz rustled the clothes, and a green belt dropped and draped itself over Heather's shoulder. "Yes, here it is. Nice and clean." She hung the shirt on the doorknob. "It's almost time for dinner, Heather. I'll call you as soon as it's ready."

Heather sighed as her mother closed first the closet door, leaving her in the dark, and then the door to her room, leaving her all alone. She could hear her mother going back downstairs. The flashlight went out, and Heather shook it back to life. Then she turned it off to sit there in the blackness. This must be how I felt when I was a baby, she thought. All safe, and warm, and close. But she wasn't a baby, and she remembered again how she was growing.

She thought of all the school pictures she'd ever been in, and slid from her warm nest, out of the closet, and over to her bookcase. She pulled her album off the bottom shelf and put it on her bed. Kindergarten, first grade, second, third, fourth. Each class picture was taped on a page, one after the other. Each showed her growing bigger and bigger.

In the first picture she had curly sticking-out pigtails that were held by little barrettes with colored balls. She was sitting in the front row, one sock up, one sock down. In the next picture her hair was short, a mass of curls all around her head, but she was still in the front row, one sock up and one sock down.

There was a knock on her door, and Samantha poked her head in. "I need your dictionary," she said.

"No," Heather answered. "Use your own."

Samantha walked into the room. "What are you looking at? Your old school pictures?"

"Yeah."

Samantha knelt down beside her and put her hand over her eyes. "I'll bet I can find you," she said. "You're sitting in the front row, with one sock up, and the other down." Then she looked closely at the picture. "There you are! Front row, and what did I tell you?"

Heather couldn't help but laugh.

"This year you'll have to stand in the back row," Sam said.

"Nah. I don't want to do that. I like being in the front. I'm one of the littlest in the class. I'm glad. I don't want to grow too fast." Heather looked carefully at last year's picture. She was wearing her hair in a neat ponytail, with bangs. That's exactly how she'd wear it this year. See, she hadn't changed at all.

"That's silly," said Sam. "You've got to grow."

"Not me. I'm staying this way for a while. I like nine."

"You can't do that," Sam told her. "Your birthday's next week."

Heather slammed the album shut and glared at her.

"C'mon, lend me your dictionary," Sam demanded.

"I told you to use your own."

"But I can't find it."

"Look under the forty tons of stuff all over your floor. I'll bet you it's there someplace."

"Thanks for nothing, you obnoxious *ex-*

*position*," Sam said, slamming the door behind her.

"Yeah, you'd *better* find your dictionary," Heather muttered.

Heather's mother's voice boomed into the hallway. "Dinner, girls." She was calling up in the speaking tube that led from the kitchen to the second floor. Heather could hear Sam thudding down the steps. Gently she closed her album and left it on her bed. She could too stay nine if she wanted to.

Sam and her mother were already at the table when she got to the kitchen, and her favorite dinner was on the counter—a big white box: pizza. Her mother gave her a slice and looked at her carefully.

"Don't your eyes hurt, reading in the dark like that, dear?"

"No, I could do that for hours," she answered.

"Yeah, but she wasn't reading when I was in there," Sam teased, sprinkling oregano on her slice. "She was admiring herself in all her old school pictures."

Heather ignored Sam and took a bite of the point of her pizza slice. Cheese stretched from her mouth to the slice, and she reached her arms out farther and farther, making the strings grow until they snapped and draped down over her chin. It was burning hot, so she took a cool drink of her milk and slipped from her chair. "Too hot," she said, positioning herself in the doorway and boosting herself up.

Up Heather went, as quick as a woodpecker up the side of a tree. She paused at the top and counted the slices of pizza left.

"Look at her," Sam muttered. "What are you, the human fly? Don't you think you're getting too big for that?"

"I'll never get too big for this," Heather told her.

"Oh, no? Can you see yourself as a grown-up, a famous scientist, or an editor of a news-paper. 'Oh, excuse me, gentlemen,' "—Sam made her voice high and silly—" 'I just have to climb the walls for a minute. I'll be right back.' "

"Ma! Make her stop!"

"That's enough now, both of you," her mother said, tapping her chair. "Come sit down here and finish eating."

"My slice is too hot."

"It's true, Mom, isn't it?" Sam asked. "She won't be able to do that when she's all grown up, will she?"

"Probably not." Her mother shrugged. "*I* can't do it."

"Well, *I'll* be able to do it!" Heather shouted.

"Oh, yeah? You won't do it for a while, and then one day you'll try and suddenly you'll realize your legs got just a little too long, or you got just a little too heavy, and it won't work anymore."

"Oh, no," Heather said calmly now from her high perch. "I'm going to do it every day, every *single* day, and I'll be able to do it every day because I did it the day before, and nobody grows too much in one day. And then even when I'm finally full size, it'll happen real slow, and I'll always be able to do it. Right, Mom?"

Her mother looked thoughtful. "Maybe. I don't know, but I do know if you don't eat, you won't have the strength to get up or down. Come sit and eat now."

After her bath, Heather laid out the clothes for the next day on her bed—the shirt like the one that Dorelle had said she would wear, the dark-gray skirt, the white tights, her light-gray shoes, the pink barrette. They looked nice lying there on the bed. She pulled the shirt on over her head and admired herself in the mirror that hung on her closet door. She pulled on her skirt, which looked stupid without the tights, so she put on her tights too, to see it all together. There, it was perfect. Then she pulled her hair back in a ponytail and checked herself against the picture in her scrapbook one more time.

Last year she had worn her striped skirt and her red sweater. She tried to decide what to do. Should she wear the shirt she had promised Dorelle she would wear, so they could be twins? Or should she wear exactly what she wore last year, to prove she hadn't changed at all? She went to her closet and searched. She hadn't worn the striped skirt all year, but it was still there. The red sweater was in her drawer. She stood there thinking. And then she knew what she had to do. Heather pulled off everything she had on and made the switch.

There. In the mirror she was exactly the same as last year, no doubt about it. The skirt was a wee bit shorter, and the sleeves on the sweater looked tight, but it was fine. She had even put socks on and pushed one down and one up. Heather smiled at herself. Perfect. And so that she wouldn't have to spend more time in the morning getting dressed again, Heather climbed right into bed, dressed for picture taking.

"Good night, Heather," her mother said, peeking into the room.

" 'Night, Mom," Heather answered, from deep inside the blankets that were pulled up over her head.

"No kiss?" her mother asked.

Heather stuck her face out of the blankets

for a kiss. Her mother was smiling. "Doing your old baby trick, under the covers to-night?"

"Yup," Heather said, smiling at her mother. They kissed good night, and her mother put the light out. Then Heather pulled the cover back over her head, making everything dark and quiet, and she breathed in the softness of being little again.

# 3
# Class-Picture-Taking Day

Heather put the chewable vitamin right on the side of her mouth, over the tooth that was loose, and she bit hard, making it pinch.

"But I thought you and Dorelle were going to wear the same outfits," her mother was saying. "Didn't you say you wanted to look like twins? Same clothes? Same hairdo?"

Heather took a mouthful of scrambled eggs. "I changed my mind," she said.

"But Heather, those clothes have been in your closet for months. I can't remember the last time you wore them. And they look all wrinkled, like you slept in them!"

"These clothes fit me just fine. I haven't worn them in a while, but I haven't grown at all since the last time. It's what I want to wear." Heather kept eating, hoping her mother wouldn't force her to change and ruin everything.

"What about Dorelle?" her mother asked, taking a different view. "Isn't she expecting you to wear—"

"Ma!" Sam looked up suddenly from her homework notes that were spread out across the breakfast table, scattering cereal onto the floor. "You have to let her wear what she feels good in," she said. "This is a sign of growing interference."

"I think you mean growing *independence*," Mrs. Fitz said, pouring herself a cup of coffee and tapping meaningfully on the dictionary that was propped up in front of Sam. Then she turned back to Heather with a puzzled expression. "Well, I guess it *is* up to you, dear. It's just I think it's silly to wear old clothes to have your picture taken, especially when you already promised somebody—"

"No, Ma, it's growing *interference*," Sam said, pointing to a page in the dictionary. "It says here, 'Interference: taking part in other people's affairs without invitation.' "

Heather smiled a little and kept her head down.

"Well, excuse me!" their mother said, narrowing her eyes at Sam. "If I get in the way around here, you'll let me know, won't you?"

"No problem," Sam answered as she got up, stacking her books and taking a last drink of her juice. "You will be *notarized* if you get in the way."

"Notified," Mrs. Fitz corrected, clearing off the table brusquely. "Now both of you get out of here, or you'll be late for the halls of academia."

"Halls of academia?" Sam stared at her mother.

"Look it up," Mrs. Fitz said in a clipped voice. "Not now!" she fussed, when Sam sat down again. Mrs. Fitz put the dictionary back in the pile and eased Sam toward the door. "Come on, Heather," she added. "It's time to pack up and leave. You don't want to be late for the photographer."

It was a cold, gray day, and Heather walked along quickly with her backpack over her shoulders and her hands thrust into her pockets. She was feeling pretty good, satisfied with herself and content. In a word, she was feeling nine. She was holding on to nine without any problem at all. No problem, that is, until she got to the school yard and saw Dorelle waiting for her at the front gate.

"I thought you'd *never* get here," Dorelle called, waving her hand, and then her wave stopped in midair. Her smile vanished. "Your hair! You said you'd wear it loose today. You said you'd just let it be curly."

Heather smoothed her hand along the side of her head, pushing any stray strands back toward her ponytail. She felt a little uneasy.

"I changed my mind, and it was late by the time I decided, so I couldn't call you."

"What do you mean you changed your mind?" Dorelle's face looked angry and tight. Her hair wasn't naturally curly like Heather's, and Heather could tell Dorelle's mother had probably set it the night before. It curled all over the place, framing her squinting eyes and her furious mouth.

Heather looked off into the distance, staring at the kids who were chasing each other across the school yard. She shrugged. She didn't know what to say. She didn't know how to explain it. After all, Dorelle had turned ten a few months ago. She'd had a skating party, and Dorelle had even whispered to Heather that she almost felt like a teenager now that she had two digits in her age. How do you explain staying nine and not changing to someone like that? Heather shrugged and looked back at her friend. "I don't know. I just changed my mind. I decided to wear the same thing I wore for last year's picture."

Dorelle's mouth fell open. "The same thing?

You're wearing the same thing, the exact same thing as *last* year?"

Heather nodded. It still didn't sound at all stupid to her. What was the big deal?

Dorelle's face grew small and mean. "I should have been twins with Lauren," she said slowly. "I never should have been twins with you!" And at that Dorelle turned and walked away from Heather. Heather could see her dark skirt, and her white tights, the gray shoes, and the little pink barrette in her hair.

I guess I should have called, she thought with an awful sinking feeling inside; and letting the backpack slide down her arms, she grabbed the straps with her hands. The school bell rang and she headed for her classroom.

Mrs. Kleintoch was waiting at the door, and Heather had to look at her twice. Was it really Mrs. Kleintoch? She had blue eye shadow on her lids and a sparkly earring showing through her hair beneath each ear. She patted Heather's shoulder as she passed, and Heather noticed the red nail polish and the unfamiliar perfume.

"Let's hurry, people," she was saying. "We

have a lot to do today, and we're the first class to be photographed, so we need to get our things in order and line up right away."

Everyone was beginning to line up, and Heather looked around. Dorelle was whispering to Lauren over by the pencil sharpener. Heather looked away. And then she saw Sonya. Sonya's desk was right next to Heather's, and she usually wore her hair kind of plain, but today she had about three hundred little braids all over her head, and at the end of each braid was a tiny bead.

"Oh, your hair is beautiful!" Heather said, delicately touching the beads with her fingers and seeing them clink against each other.

Sonya smiled broadly. "My mother said I could wear my hair like this when I was ten years old, for my ten-year-old picture. She would never do it before. Said it was too much trouble to do on someone so little, but now I'm old enough."

"Let's stop this, boys, right now," Mrs. Kleintoch called over their heads. Everyone turned around and looked to the back of the line. Jeremy, red-faced and wearing a white shirt and a tie, was pushing Freddie.

"He keeps pulling my tie, Mrs. Kleintoch! Tell him to leave my tie alone."

Mrs. Kleintoch walked to the back of the line. With her hand firmly on Freddie's shoulder, she whispered in his ear. Heather looked at Jeremy's tie. It was green with a little horse painted on it, a horse rearing up on its hind legs. It was weird to see Jeremy in something other than his baseball shirts.

Freddie's face clouded over as he listened to his teacher. He crossed his arms in front of him and scowled. His hair was all slicked down and shiny. Mrs. Kleintoch smoothed one of his stray hairs into place. "That's it. Now let's at least stay calm and orderly until your picture is taken. Shall we?" She smiled at the class, and everyone faced forward.

The photographer was set up for picture taking in the library as usual. He was a spry little man who ran from place to place. He ran from his camera to the benches he had lined up, back to the camera, to the door, to his equipment, all the while yelling, "Watch the wires! Please watch the wires, children!"

Mrs. Kleintoch eased them to the benches one at a time, touching each one as they passed.

"Just a minute! Just a minute! Watch the wires!" the photographer shouted. He ran to the benches and began directing everyone. "All the tall children in the back, please. There you go. Standing. I want all the tall children standing behind the benches." He directed and pointed and poked until the whole class was jammed together either behind or on the benches. Heather sat on the first bench next to Sonya. With one foot she felt to make sure her one sock was down, and she pulled the other one up tight.

The photographer peered into his camera at them, and Heather smiled. "Just a minute," he said. "We need some adjustments." First he would peer in the camera and then he would look around at them. "You in the green shirt," he'd say. "Change places with the boy at the end. That's better. That's good. Now you, with the glasses, come in closer."

Heather yawned and just sat there. She glanced at Sonya's clinking beads.

"And you. You in the red sweater."

She wondered how Sonya's mother made such tiny little braids like that.

"Heather!" the whole class shouted at once.

Heather was startled.

"Yes, you," the photographer said. "You in the red sweater, I want you to stand in the back next to the boy with the tie."

"But I'm short," she said.

"You're taller than everyone on the bench," he told her, motioning with his arm where to go.

Heather took her place at the end of the back row. She couldn't believe it. Standing in the back row! She wasn't tall enough for the back row, and nobody would see her socks from back here.

The photographer ran to his camera and peered inside once again. "Beautiful," he said.

"Now I want everyone to say 'Frank Sinatra.' "

There was dead silence except for Mrs. Kleintoch, who sang right out. "Frank Sinatra."

And when everyone laughed, the photographer snapped the picture.

# 4
# But It Doesn't Mean I'm Ten

Mrs. Fitz was waiting for Heather after school. The small red car was parked at the curb in the lineup of other rides home, puffs of smoke rising behind each one. Heather climbed into the backseat and collapsed as she shut the door behind her.

"So how was your day, Heather?" her mother asked, turning around and patting her on the knee. "Everything go okay?"

"It was all right." Heather didn't feel like talking. Her hair had come out of its ponytail and swirled around her face and collar in unruly curls, and her skirt was uncomfortable, too tight and itchy around her waist.

"I wonder what Mr. Gabrielle was using that ladder for," Mrs. Fitz said as she began easing her way away from the curb and out into traffic. Heather looked out at Mr. Gabrielle, the custodian, who was carrying a long awkward ladder across the school yard to the storage building.

"He had to use it in our classroom," Heather answered, remembering Mrs. Kleintoch making everyone stand back and watch quietly as Mr. Gabrielle climbed to the very top. "Jerry wore a tie today, and as soon as picture taking was over, Freddie got it away from him and threw it in the air and it got stuck on the lights."

"Sounds like an exciting day," Mrs. Fitz said. "And how did the picture taking go?" asked Mrs. Fitz. "Terrible. I had to stand in the back row. The photographer said I was one of the taller kids, and he made me stand in the back with the giants! I couldn't believe it. You probably won't even be able to see me when we get the picture. All you'll see is the top of my head."

"I doubt that, Heather. I've been noticing lately how much taller you seem. I think you're definitely getting taller."

"I'm not!" Heather said. "I'm exactly the same as last year! That photographer is just stupid. I'm just the same—same clothes and everything." Heather leaned back and squirmed, giving herself a little room in the tight skirt that was so uncomfortable when she was sitting down. "And on top of that, Dorelle won't even talk to me now that I didn't come as her twin this morning." Heather sighed and stared out the window at the bare trees. "Stupid day," she muttered to herself.

"Sounds like a good old-fashioned party might cheer you up and set things right," her mother said quietly.

Heather glared at the back of her mother's head.

"Doesn't have to be a birthday party," her mother went on. "No gifts, no singing. We could even call it an *un*birthday party, and maybe you could invite Dorelle to come. Maybe that would help smooth things over."

Heather thought about it. An unbirthday party. "What would we eat?"

"Well, I could make a lemonade cake—no number on top, of course, and no candles to blow out—and some moon cookies. Actually, moon cookies in November is a Chinese tradition . . . seems I heard that somewhere before . . . nothing to do with a birthday at all. We could have the party Sunday night, and never mention it's your birthday, and we could ask Grandma and Grandpa to come, and maybe Uncle Lou and his girlfriend—"

"Rosa Rita?"

"Uh-huh."

"I like her," Heather said, thinking hard. She thought of Rosa Rita and her funny clothes, the armful of fluorescent bracelets, and her wild hair. And her makeup. She was really good with makeup, all shades of colors between her eye and her eyebrow. Maybe Rosa Rita would put makeup on Heather and Dorelle for the night, so they could see what they'd look like when they grew up. Not that Heather really cared about that, but Dorelle would like it. Heather knew she would. "I'll think about it," Heather said as her mother pulled into their driveway and parked by the back door. "I'll let you know later."

Heather was taking a big chance. She knew it, but she decided to try anyway. She dialed Dorelle's number. Three rings and Dorelle answered.

"Hello?"

Here goes, thought Heather. "Hello, Lady Madeline," she said, using Dorelle's secret play name.

There was total silence in the phone. Not even breathing noises.

"Hello? Are you there, Lady Madeline?"

"What do you want, Heather?"

"You have to meet me in the dungeon. It's urgent."

"I don't want to play with you," Dorelle said, a nasty edge to her voice. "I have to go call for Lauren now."

Heather felt like she was holding her nose and jumping into a freezing-cold lake. It was too late to turn back now. "Please, Lady Madeline. It's a matter of life and death. The whole kingdom could be at stake!"

"Tell me over the phone," Dorelle answered. "I don't have time to go to the dungeon."

"No. It has to be the dungeon." Heather cupped her hand over her mouth and whispered into the phone, "The dragon is listening."

"Oh, all right," Dorelle said in her grouchy voice. "But I can only stay a minute. Lauren's waiting for me." And at that she hung up.

Heather hung up the phone and slipped into her coat. Her mother was sitting right there at the kitchen table reading. "I'll just be a minute, Mom. I have to meet Dorelle by the church, and then I'll come right back."

"You can stay out awhile if you want to," Mrs. Fitz said, pulling Heather's collar out and patting it flat. "But I have two questions before you go."

"What?"

"Should I call Grandma and Grandpa about the unbirthday party Sunday night?"

"I don't know yet. I'll let you know after I talk to Dorelle. What's the other question?"

Her mother looked at her seriously. "Am I the dragon?"

Heather laughed. "Of course you are!" And she ran out the back door.

There was a small church a block from Heather's house. It was exactly as many steps from her house as it was from Dorelle's, and except for Sunday there was never anybody around. It was an old, chilly stone building, and on the side was a stairway to a basement door that looked as if it hadn't been opened in a hundred years. Old vines and brambles grew down the walls and around the latches. The steps were slate, and at the bottom in the exact center of the ground was a drain that looked like an old magic symbol. This was the dungeon. Heather got there first. She sat on the bottom step and waited, pushing little sticks into the drain. Soon she heard steps, and Dorelle came down and sat beside her.

"What do you want? Lauren's waiting for me," she said.

"I know. You told me about four hundred times already."

Dorelle glared at her.

"I wanted to know if you would come to my house Sunday night for an unbirthday party. It's my birthday but I don't want a party, because I'm not ready to be ten yet, but my mother wants to have my grandparents over, so she said we could have an unbirthday party."

"What do you mean you're not ready to be ten? Ten's fun."

"So is nine. I like nine. It's my best year."

Dorelle looked at Heather as if she were an interesting science project, sugar crystals turning all colors before her eyes. "You're weird" was all she said.

"So will you come?"

"To an unparty? You mean no presents, or food, or balloons? No birthday cards? No singing?"

"Well, we'll have a cake and food and all, but no candles, and no birthday stuff. That's all."

"No presents? You're not even going to get presents?"

"Christmas is only a month away," Heather said.

Dorelle shook her head and stood up. "I don't think so, Heather. I'm really mad at you for not being my twin today."

"But don't you understand? I had to be like last year, just the same, and not be turning ten."

A cold wind whipped down the dungeon steps and chilled them.

"Nah," said Dorelle. "I don't think I want to go."

"Rosa Rita's coming," Heather said at last.

Dorelle frowned and studied Heather. "To the unparty?"

"Yeah, and maybe I can ask her to put makeup on us, like she does, with all the different colors—"

"Do you think she'd spray our hair orange?"

"Sure!" Heather said.

Dorelle was weakening. "Do you have any of that blue nail polish left?"

"Yeah! We can do our nails before she comes, and then when we're all made up, maybe we can put on a show for everybody!"

"All right," Dorelle said, starting up the steps. "I'll come." Heather walked out of the dungeon with her, and they stood by the curb quietly. Were they friends again or weren't they? A bus went by. Two bikes. They just stood there. Finally Dorelle asked, "Wanna come to my house to make popcorn?"

"I thought you had to call for Lauren."

"I just said that to get you mad." A smile stretched across Dorelle's face. Her freckles were like bits of brown sugar sprinkled over her nose.

"Yeah, but you didn't make me mad," Heather informed her, starting up the block toward Dorelle's house. She tossed her hair over her shoulder and walked as if she were dragging a long red-velvet skirt trimmed with fur and diamonds. "Nobody can make Lady Forcynthia mad," she said in her queen voice. "That's because Lady Forcynthia never changes. She's always the same."

# 5
# The Unbirthday Party

Heather and Dorelle were in Heather's room putting on the final coat of blue nail polish when the doorbell rang. They could hear Grandpa's loud voice and Grandma laughing.

"They're here," called Sam, running past Heather's closed door and down the stairs.

"Let's wait awhile," Heather said, blowing on her fingernails and waving them in the air. "After all, it's not like there's anything special I have to get down there for." She looked at Dorelle uneasily.

"But maybe they brought presents," Dorelle said quietly.

"Mom made them promise they wouldn't."

Dorelle shrugged and lined up the nail polishes on Heather's bookcase. "Well, let's go down anyway, and see if Rosa Rita's here."

Heather's grandparents were sitting on the sofa, dressed up and fancy like they were going to a party. Heather knew she never wanted to be a grown-up, not like her grandmother was, with small brown shoes with fussy laces, and eyeglasses hanging around her neck on a sparkly blue string. For an instant Heather felt silly that Grandma and Grandpa knew about her not wanting to be ten, but they didn't say anything about it. They just asked about school and gymnastics and her flute lessons.

"Where's Uncle Lou and Rosa Rita?" Heather asked.

"They should be here any minute," her grandmother said.

"What's the big deal with Rosa Rita?" Sam wanted to know.

"Nothing," Heather said, as she heard footsteps on the front porch and then the doorbell. "They're here!" she yelled, and both she and Dorelle ran to open the door.

Uncle Lou, of all people, was carrying a present. You could never really count on him to follow directions. And Rosa Rita, well, Rosa Rita was Rosa Rita. She was wearing a long hot-pink coat, baggy green pants, a jungle blouse, and black nail polish, with a star in the center of each nail. Heather hugged them both, and Dorelle just stood there with her mouth open.

"I know it's a little early for a Christmas present," Uncle Lou said, "but I just couldn't control myself." He held out the present before him. It was wrapped in reindeer paper, with a green ribbon, and attached to the bow was a little red Christmas ball, sprinkled with glitter. Heather didn't quite know what to do.

"A Christmas present!" complained Sam. "Where's mine?"

"Your what?" Uncle Lou asked stupidly.

"My Christmas present!"

"But it's only November," he teased. "How

can I give you your Christmas present now?"

Heather took the disguised birthday present from her uncle and glanced nervously at Dorelle.

"Well, at least you got *one* present," Dorelle whispered.

Mrs. Fitz hung up the coats, and Heather and Dorelle sat on the stairs and Heather opened her present carefully, saving the ball and the ribbon. A WORLD OF WEALTH said the lettering on the box. Inside was a small globe of the earth on a stand, and on top of the globe was a slot. It was a bank. And Heather could hear there were already a few coins inside.

"Thank you, Uncle Lou," she yelled from the stairs.

"What is it, Heather?" her mother called from the living room.

"A bank," she answered, not moving from where she was.

"Let's see it," her mother ordered.

Heather rolled her eyes and walked to the doorway. She never wanted to be a grown-up like her mother either, always wanting to know every little thing. Heather braced herself. Now they would start about her birthday. But they didn't. Grandpa wanted to put some money in her bank, and then Grandma did, while Sam scowled at Heather from across the room. Then Heather stopped in front of Rosa Rita, the bank in her hand.

"Wanna see my makeup collection?" Heather asked.

Rosa Rita smiled. "Sure."

"You have to come up to my room."

Rosa Rita laughed. "Okay. Sounds like fun."

Heather clasped Rosa Rita's hand and called over her shoulder as she led her out of the room. "We'll see you in a little bit. We'll be upstairs."

Rosa Rita shrugged and waved to Uncle Lou as she was swept out of the living room and up the steps to Heather's bedroom. Heather and Dorelle had lined up all the old eye shadows and blushes and pencils and lipsticks on the bed. There was also a box of tissues, a towel, and a mirror that made everything look gigantic, especially noses. Heather placed her new bank on her pillow.

"Wow," said Rosa Rita, leaning over the bed and touching the tubes and small boxes. "You have enough makeup here to do a fashion spread in *Vogue*."

Heather smiled proudly. "Do I have enough for you to do me and Dorelle?"

"Now?" asked Rosa Rita. "Tonight?"

They nodded and smiled at her expectantly.

She hesitated for just a minute. "Oh, all right. Let's see if we can transform you and surprise everyone. Just make sure you wash your face real good tonight, you hear? Get it all off before you go to school tomorrow."

"We will," Dorelle promised. "Cross our hearts."

"All right, then. Dorelle, you first. Heather, you be my assistant, and give me what I need."

Rosa Rita sat down on the floor with Dorelle in front of her. They crossed their legs like Indians. Rosa Rita put the towel around Dorelle's neck, pushed her hair back away from her eyes, and studied her face. Heather watched carefully. It probably wouldn't be too bad to be a grown-up like Rosa Rita, with fun clothes and makeup and such an easy way about her.

"Hmmm," Rosa Rita said quietly. She ran her fingers over Dorelle's cheekbones and down her nose. "Do you have some green shadow there?" she asked.

As quick as she could, Heather had three shades of green before her. Rosa Rita picked one out and began shading Dorelle's eye carefully with the little brush and smoothing with her fingers. Dorelle sat as still as stone, her eyes closed and her face turned up.

"How about silver?" Rosa Rita asked. "We need a little silver."

"Silver?" Heather stared at her collection. She never even knew they made silver. "No. I don't have silver. I ran out."

"Well, run down and bring my pocketbook up to me. I think I have some."

Heather was out the door like lightning and down the steps. She burst into the living room.

"Where's Rosa Rita's pocketbook?" she asked. It was next to Uncle Lou, and he held it out to her.

"What are you doing up there?" Uncle Lou asked.

"Nothing," Heather answered, and ran back up the steps. "Here you go." She placed the pocketbook next to Rosa Rita, who turned it upside down on the rug and spilled its contents out like a treasure chest. Heather gasped with joy. Colors and scents and tubes and compacts and brushes and combs and sprays! Dorelle and Heather stared in amazement.

"Here it is," Rosa Rita said quietly, picking a large silver tube out of the pile. She pulled it open, and it glittered like starshine. Rosa Rita held it to Dorelle's eye and slowly and carefully drew a thick line across her lid.

"Oh, it's *beautiful!*" Heather said. Rosa Rita did the other eye, going back and forth, matching them carefully and smoothing the green and the silver until Dorelle's eyes looked like wild creatures from Ed's Aquarium. Then she brushed blush on Dorelle's cheeks and her ears and down her nose, put lipstick on her lips with her little finger, and brushed her straight, stringy hair backward till it stood up all around her head; and then as a final finishing touch she pulled a can from her pile and sprayed her hair. Instantly Dorelle's hair was dusted with sparkles, a million glistening sparkles that made her hair shine and shimmer and catch the light when she moved.

Dorelle was spectacular. The three of them stared into the mirror. "Perfect," Rosa Rita decided. "Do you like it?"

"Yeah! It's great!" Dorelle tried to see her closed eyelids in the mirror, pouted her lips, and turned her head from side to side.

"Now do me," Heather pleaded. She was already sitting in place, her hair pulled back, her face ready. Rosa Rita squinted at her. "I have an idea I want to try on you," she said slowly. "It might take a little longer, but it will be worth it. Can you sit very still?"

"Sure."

There was a knock on Heather's door. "Can I come in?" It was Uncle Lou.

"No!" Heather shouted. "Not yet. We'll tell you when."

"Ro?"

"Don't worry, Lou," Rosa Rita assured him. "We'll be down in a little while."

They giggled together as they heard his footsteps disappear down the stairs. Rosa Rita held Heather's face in her hands and studied her. Heather closed her eyes. "I hear you're skipping your birthday this year," Rosa Rita said softly. Heather's eyes flew open and she stared at her, saying nothing. "I know just how you feel."

"You do?"

Dorelle lay on the floor next to them, the new globe bank balanced on her chest. "I don't understand at all," Dorelle offered. "Why would someone want to stay nine?"

Rosa Rita was drawing something on Heather's face with a blue pencil. Heather watched her eyes and listened. "Well, you know what happened to me? I have a lot of brothers and sisters—"

"How many?"

"Eight. So what happened was they actually just forgot my birthday one year. My twelfth birthday went right by. When my mother finally thought of it, she was so upset. But you know what? I was glad. I figured I got to be eleven awhile longer while no one was watching. I loved being eleven."

"Like I love nine!" Heather said, her face lighting up.

"But how old are you now?" Dorelle asked Rosa Rita.

"Twenty-three, or twenty-two, if you don't count that year we all skipped."

"But you didn't stay eleven," Dorelle pointed out.

"Well, I stayed eleven awhile, but then, I don't know, I just knew I was twelve one day. But I don't think I was twelve very long, maybe just half a year, and then I was thirteen. Thirteen I liked! My mother let me wear mascara then."

"She did?" both girls said together.

"Yep. Then things really started opening up for me. High school, art classes . . . Now every year is a good year."

Heather thought about that.

Dorelle was listening while lying on the floor, squinting up into the bank's slot and shaking it in the air over her head. The coins rattled. "That's just what I—" Suddenly some coins slid out of the slot, showering onto Dorelle's face, and then unexpectedly she was choking. Rosa Rita dropped the makeup and pulled Dorelle to sit up. Heather could barely think.

"What's wrong?" she asked.

Dorelle looked frightened. Rosa Rita was talking to her, her hand gently on her back. "Can't you breathe?" Rosa Rita was asking.

But Dorelle couldn't even talk. Her face was growing red, and before Heather could think of what to do, Rosa Rita had pulled Dorelle up and had whisked her around so her back was toward Rosa Rita. Then she put her arms around Dorelle, making a fist with one hand, and with a sudden jerk she squeezed below Dorelle's ribs. At first nothing happened. "It's okay, it's okay," Rosa Rita was saying. Then she squeezed again.

A funny popping sound came from Dorelle, and a coin shot out of her mouth and across the room, dropping into Heather's pile of stuffed animals. Dorelle started coughing and breathing hard.

"Are you okay?" Heather asked, feeling all weak inside.

"Yeah," whispered Dorelle, her voice all shaky and scratchy. Rosa Rita was patting her gently and watching her face.

"That was a close call," she said. "You scared the life out of me."

"But you knew just what to do, Rosa Rita. You saved her life," Heather said. She watched Rosa Rita carefully, knowing that if she had been alone with Dorelle, she wouldn't have known what to do. But Rosa Rita knew— Rosa Rita, with her funny clothes and her face like an art project, knew exactly what to do. Heather loved her. Rosa Rita was just the kind of grown-up that Heather wanted to be.

Quietly, thoughtfully, Heather began digging in her pile of stuffed animals. "I think the coin flew in here someplace," she mumbled. "What was it, Dorelle? A quarter? A dime?"

Dorelle frowned. "I didn't look at it before it dropped down my throat, Heather."

"Here it is! A nickel!"

Rosa Rita took Heather's hand and pulled her back down to the floor. "Come on, you two. Let's get back to work. And from now on, let's keep the silver on your lids, not down your throats. Is it a deal?"

Heather and Dorelle both agreed, and Heather could see herself laughing in the mirror, and all around one of her eyes was a gigantic blue star.

# 6
# One Step at a Time

"Is everybody ready?" Heather shouted from the top of the stairway. Rosa Rita had started down ahead of them, and Heather and Dorelle stood side by side, clutching each other's hands.

"Ready for what?" her grandfather called back.

"For anything!" she answered. "Anything and everything!"

Sam was at the bottom of the steps. "What are you up to?" she asked, peering up into the darkness at the top. "Oh, I don't believe it," she muttered as the two of them came into view.

They marched down the steps into the living room and twirled around for all to see. Dorelle's hair sparkled and rained glitter on her shoulders as she turned, and Heather's starry eye flashed in the center of her blue star.

"Beautiful!"

"Incredible!"

"Spectacular!"

Everyone applauded and called out admiring words.

"Impostuous," Sam muttered from the doorway.

"I think you should put on a show for us," Grandpa said. "Maybe a little entertainment would be in order."

"Well, before the entertainment," Heather's mother began, "let's have some coffee and cake, okay?" She took Heather's face between her two hands and looked at her carefully. "That's amazing, Heather," she said wistfully. "A star on my Moon face." Heather could see her mother's eyes were getting a little bright.

"Aw, Ma, cut it out."

"Cake, everybody!" her mother called out, turning toward the kitchen.

They all gathered in the dining room, taking their places at the table. Normally, for a regular birthday, Heather would have sat at the head of the table, her back to the window that looked out into the backyard through the bare cherry tree. But tonight she sat in her usual seat, nothing special about her.

"I guess you can't climb the walls anymore, Heather, huh?" Uncle Lou winked at her across the table. "Too big, right?"

"I can still do it," Heather answered, flashing him a look. She wasn't too big for anything. She slipped from her chair and positioned herself in the doorway between the dining room and the kitchen. Up she slid, hands, feet, hands, feet, until she was at the top.

"Well, look at that, would you?" Grandpa was grinning up at her.

"Oh, be careful," Grandma said, her hands

covering her mouth nervously. "You shouldn't be doing that, Heather. It looks too dangerous."

Heather didn't listen to her. She just stayed in her perch, pressed high in the doorway, as safe as a spider. Her mother passed beneath her with the lemonade cake. It was high and pink and delicious-looking, and there were no candles on it, and no big number. If she had celebrated this year, they would have needed two numbers, one and zero. It was just as well, thought Heather, watching the cake go by. It looked all right without numbers.

"She won't be able to do that much longer," Sam said. "Only nine-year-olds can do that. It's crash-on-your-headsville when you turn ten and try to climb the walls. Something like that can't go on forever, you know."

"I don't know about that," Grandpa mused. "When I was a boy, living on my parents' farm, a calf was born, and I thought if I lifted him every day, every single morning, that he would grow bigger all the time, but I would match him with my strength and be able to lift him even when he was a full-grown bull."

They were all looking at him. "What happened?" Heather asked, sliding down the door and coming to stand by him. "Could you do it?" she asked hopefully.

"Well, every morning I'd go out to the barn before he ate, wrap my arms around his legs, and lift him, even walk with him a bit before I'd put him down." Grandpa sat there, remembering.

"And?" Sam asked, impatient. "What happened?"

"I don't know," he answered, genuinely puzzled. "I think baseball season started or something, and I forgot about it, and next thing I knew, the darn thing was bigger than I was."

"Oh, Grandpa," Sam said, disappointed.

"But I still believe," he continued, "that if I'd kept with it, and lifted that calf every day, I could have lifted a grown bull—"

Grandpa stopped talking suddenly, and his full attention was on Rosa Rita, who was standing in the doorway between the kitchen and the dining room. They all turned to see what he was staring at. She had kicked off her short boots and was peeling off her fluorescent socks, one pink, one orange. No one said a word. Heather held her breath and watched. Pressing her hands against the doorway and giving herself a little boost, Rosa Rita pushed her bare feet against the moldings and edged her way to the top of the doorway. Rosa Rita was climbing the walls.

"Well, I'll be," Grandpa whispered. "Look at that. See? It *is* possible. I bet I could have lifted that bull!"

"Rosa Rita!" Uncle Lou cried, his hands slapping his head in wonder. He stared up at her in dumb surprise.

Rosa Rita smiled down at him, at all of them. "Well, Heather," she said, "what do you think?"

Heather walked over to the doorway and stood staring up at Rosa Rita. "I'm astonished," Heather said quietly.

Sam moaned. "Astonished. Give me a break. Somebody, quick, get my dictionary."

Rosa Rita's hands and her feet were planted firmly in the doorway. She and Heather looked at each other, held each other in a secret knowing.

"How old did you say you were?" Heather almost whispered.

"Twenty-three," Rosa Rita answered. "What do you say, Starface? Want to try being ten? There's nothing to it. There's no big change, nothing's really different. You're still you. You can still do all the same things."

Everyone was very quiet, waiting.

Heather felt as if she were standing in the center of the wooden seesaw at school trying to keep both seats evenly balanced in the air, weighing this side and then that, uncertain. At last she turned and faced her mother. "Well . . . all right. I'll be ten."

Everyone applauded, even Sam. "But I'm stopping at twenty-three," Heather added, and they all laughed.

"Wait!" Heather cried, holding up her hands. "What time is it?"

"Seven forty," her mother said without even

looking at the clock in the hall. She had known all along.

Ideas were cooking behind Heather's star eye. A glimmer of a devilish smile passed over her face. "Come on, Dorelle! We're going to put on a show!" And she ran out of the dining room and up the stairs, with Dorelle following.

"Heather!" her mother called after her. "The cake! Come have some cake first!"

"Put some candles on it!" Heather called from upstairs.

Then everyone just waited expectantly. Heather's mother pressed ten candles and one for good luck into the pink icing, and then two number candles, a one and a zero, that she had bought just in case, and then she took her seat. Soon Dorelle came running down the steps and checked the clock. Seven forty-four.

"Ladies and gentlemen," she began. "We're going to have a birthday countdown. Come to the doorway and join in the fun." Everyone got up, moved to the wide arched doorway of the dining room, and stared up the long stairway.

"Have you got my sleeping bag up there?" Sam asked, knowing what was about to happen.

"Oh, no, Heather, you're not going to—" her mother whispered, looking nervously at Heather's grandmother.

Uncle Lou put his arm around Rosa Rita's shoulder.

"In fifteen seconds," Dorelle began, "wall-climbing, star-faced Heather Fitz will be officially ten years old. Are you ready, Heather?"

"Ready!" came the answer.

Everyone joined in the countdown. "Ten! Nine! Eight! Seven! Six! Five! Four! Three! Two! One!"

Then suddenly, before anyone knew what was happening, Heather came shooting down the thickly carpeted stairs, lying down and wrapped in a slippery nylon sleeping bag. She was like the apple dropping in Times Square on New Year's Eve. She was like a slippery seal sliding down a shoot into its pool. "Ta-

da!" she sang at the bottom. The sleeping bag fell away as she stood up and took her bow. The star around her eye was made a little lopsided by her smiling cheeks.

"Good Lord," her grandmother muttered. "It's a wonder you've made it to ten."

"It's seven forty-five!" Heather announced. "I'm ten! It's my birthday! Bring on the cake, and the candles! Don't forget the candles!"

"I brought some balloons, just in case," Uncle Lou said, pulling the limp, brightly colored balloons from his jacket pocket. "But first," he added, turning to Rosa Rita, "I'd really like to see this twenty-three-year-old slide down the steps in a sleeping bag."

"Maybe after the cake," she teased him, and Heather and her mother led everyone back to the dining-room table, where the candles were burning brightly on the pink cake that sat in the center of the table. Heather stood next to her mother and noticed once more how she came to her mother's shoulder these days.

"You're not going to cry now, are you,

Mom?" Heather asked, looking up into her mother's face.

"Of course I am," her mother answered, slipping her arm around Heather. But she smiled. "What did you expect from an old dragon like me?"

And at that, the lights went off, leaving the burning candles shining bright in Heather's eyes, and Grandpa began to sing "Happy Birthday" a little off key. Everyone joined in, while Heather made a wish—a wish for them all to stay exactly like they were for a million years—and then she blew out the candles with one mighty blow.